THE TWELVE MONTHS

Rafe Martin

Vladyana Langer Krykorka

Stoddart Kids

TORONTO • NEW YORK

Published in Canada in 2000 by
Stoddart Kids,
a division of Stoddart Publishing Co. Limited
34 Lesmill Road
Toronto, ON M3B 2T6
Tel (416) 445-3333 Fax (416) 445-5967
E-mail cservice@genpub.com

Published in the United States in 2001 by
Stoddart Kids,
a division of Stoddart Publishing Co. Limited
180 Varick Street, 9th Floor
New York, New York 10014
Toll free 1-800-805-1083
E-mail gdsinc@genpub.com

Distributed in Canada by
General Distribution Services
325 Humber College Blvd.,
Toronto, ON M9W 7C3
Tel (416) 213-1919 Fax (416) 213-1917
E-mail cservice@genpub.com

Distributed in the United States by
General Distribution Services
4500 Witmer Industrial Estates, PMB 128
Niagara Falls, New York 14305-1386
Toll free 1-800-805-1083
E-mail gdsinc@genpub.com

Canadian Cataloguing in Publication Data

Martin, Rafe, 1946-
The twelve months

ISBN 0-7737-3249-7

1. Fairy tales – Czechoslovakia. I. Krykorka, Vladyana. II. Title.
PZ8.M44753Tw 2000   j398.2'09437   C00-931091-6

*A retelling of a Slavic "Cinderella" tale in which a young girl is given
impossible tasks to perform by her cruel aunt and cousin. By virtue of her
sweet nature she is helped and rewarded by the twelve months.*

THE CANADA COUNCIL | LE CONSEIL DES ARTS
FOR THE ARTS | DU CANADA
SINCE 1957 | DEPUIS 1957

*We acknowledge for their financial support of our
publishing program the Canada Council, the Ontario Arts
Council, and the Government of Canada through the
Book Publishing Industry Development Program (BPIDP).*

Printed and bound in Hong Kong, China

To the Twelve Months
and the mysterious seasons of our lives.
— R.M.

To Kathryn Cole, for making my dream come true.
— V.L.K.

In our village, there was once a girl named Marushka, whose mother and father had both died. She lived with her aunt and her cousin, a girl of her own age, named Holena. Their cottage sat by the edge of the forest at the foot of the mountain, and their lives could have been filled with peace.

But the aunt and the cousin were hard-hearted and made Marushka do all the work. "Sweep, Marushka!" they would shout. "Spin, Marushka!" they would yell. "Sew, Marushka!" they would laugh. "Weave, Marushka! Chop the wood! Milk the cows! Cut the hay and stack it — Marushka!"

No matter how hard the girl worked, they were never satisfied. "It's not good enough!" they would shout. "Cut it neater! Stack it higher! Sweep it cleaner!" Somehow Marushka bore it. She even found pleasure in her work. Cutting the hay, she felt the sun's good warmth and the freshening breeze. Milking the cows, she heard the wind rustling the leaves. Spinning the thread, she noticed its beauty. And as she delighted in these good gifts of nature, her own beauty grew.

...she felt the sun's good warmth and the freshening breeze.

The aunt and cousin became grumpier. All their yelling and scolding left deep lines and wrinkles in their faces.

"No one will ever want to marry me while she's around," whined Holena to her mother. So they plotted to rid themselves of Marushka.

One midwinter's day, Holena turned to her cousin and said, "Bring me some violets, fresh and sweet-scented. Do it now, you lazy good-for-nothing!"

"But how can I find violets in winter?" protested Marushka. "Violets do not bloom in snow!"

"Silence!" shouted her aunt. "Do you dare to disobey? Off with you. And don't return without those violets!"

As Marushka lifted her shawl, Holena roughly shoved her out into the cold, slammed the door behind her, and locked it.

...Holena roughly shoved her out into the cold...

Marushka made her way into the forest. The snow lay deep. She walked and walked. The ground rose beneath her feet when she reached the mountain. On and on she climbed, higher and higher. The wind howled and darkness fell. How Marushka shivered and shook. Never in all her life had she felt so lost, so lonely. Then, up ahead she saw a light and headed toward its glow.

There, on the highest peak of the mountain, a fire was burning. Around that fire sat twelve men. Three had long, white hair. Three were middle-aged, three were young, and three were still boys. They each sat on a solid block of stone. The fire crackled. No one said a word.

There, on the highest peak of the mountain...

Marushka was frightened, but the light from the flames drew her closer and gave her courage. "Good men," she said. "My name is Marushka. May I warm myself by your fire?"

The oldest of the twelve was seated on the largest block of stone, and in his hand he held a silver wand. He looked at her kindly and answered, "Of course, child. Come close, don't be afraid. We are the twelve months of the year. I am January, the first month, and so, the eldest. Tell us what brings you here. What do you seek?"

"Sir," said Marushka, approaching the warmth of the fire, "I am looking for violets."

"Dear child!" exclaimed January. "It is not the season for violets. Surely you must know this."

"Oh, January," cried Marushka. "I have been given this task by my aunt and cousin. They told me I *must* bring them violets or they will not let me return home. Please tell me, if any of you know, where I might find some."

"May I warm myself by your fire?"

January arose. Slowly he circled the fire until he stood before one of the elder men. "Brother March," he said, handing him the wand, "rise and take my place."

March rose, moved to the great block of stone, and waved the wand. At once, the flames leapt up and grew bright. The snow began to melt, and as it did, the brown earth and green grass appeared. On the trees, buds formed, opened, and unfurled. Where the icy drifts had lain, there was a meadow blue with violets!

"Gather them quickly, Marushka," said March.

Joyfully, Marushka ran into the meadow and standing among the green grasses, picked an armful of violets. "Thank you, Twelve Months!" she exclaimed with a bow. Then she ran back down the snow-covered mountain and through the frozen woods.

"Thank you, Twelve Months!"

"Let me in!" shouted Marushka above the howling wind, as she pounded on the cottage door. "Let me in! I have brought violets!"

"Go away, silly girl!" shouted Holena and her mother. "Violets do not grow in the snow."

"Open the door," cried Marushka, "and see for yourselves."

The door was opened, just a crack. Then it was flung wide. Holena and her mother looked out, their eyes bulging with surprise, and in Marushka ran. The fragrance of violets filled the house.

"Where did you get such flowers?" asked Holena.

"On the mountaintop," replied Marushka.

"Hmmmph!" Holena grabbed the flowers from Marushka and took them with no word of thanks.

"Let me in!" shouted Marushka above the howling wind...

The very next day Holena called Marushka to her again and said, "Go fetch me strawberries from the mountaintop. Make sure they are sweet and ripe."

"But strawberries can't grow in snow!" exclaimed Marushka.

"If violets can grow in the winter's snow," said Holena, "so can strawberries. Go to your mountaintop and find some. And do it now, stupid girl." Holena and her mother pushed Marushka out into the snow, and locked the door behind her once more.

"Go fetch me strawberries from the mountaintop."

Again, Marushka climbed up the mountainside, through the freezing, deep snow and howling wind, until she reached the top. When she came to where the twelve months sat, she called out, "Oh, good men, may I warm myself at your fire? My aunt and cousin have cast me out, and I am so very cold."

Once more, January raised his head and said kindly, "Come closer, child. Warm yourself. Tell us what you seek."

"They have sent me for strawberries in winter," sighed Marushka.

"They must know that strawberries do not grow in snow," said January.

"They do not care," replied Marushka. "They will not let me return unless I bring them strawberries. Please, do you know where I might find some?"

... January raised his head and said kindly ...

January rose from the great stone on which he sat and walked slowly around the circle. Placing the silver wand in June's hand he said, "Brother, go and sit in the high place."

June smiled, rose, and strode to the empty seat. He waved the wand over the fire and the flames leapt up and grew bright. At once the snow was gone and green grass grew. Leaves opened on the trees and birds flew, singing overhead. It was summer, and ripe strawberries dangled near Marushka's feet.

"Go, my dear," said June kindly. "Gather your strawberries."

Marushka picked the berries, filling her apron with them, until the red juice stained her fingers. "Thank you, Twelve Months!" she exclaimed. Then she bowed, and ran back down the snow-covered mountain to her home.

"Brother, go and sit in the high place."

"Let me in!" cried Marushka. "I have strawberries!"

The door opened a bit. Then Holena and her mother gasped, flinging the door wide. "Where did you find strawberries?" they demanded, as they grabbed the fruit and stuffed their mouths, saving not a single berry for Marushka.

"Why, up on the mountaintop," answered Marushka.

"Of course," they sniggered as they elbowed each other slyly. "On the mountaintop."

A few days later they came to Marushka again and said, "Now get us apples! Fresh, crisp, red ones. And don't return without them!"

"But bare trees grow no apples!" exclaimed Marushka.

"Don't argue, you bad girl!" they shouted. "Do as you are told!" And again, Holena and her mother drove Marushka from the cottage. "Now," they said, "we are rid of her once and for all. She will never return."

"Where did you find strawberries?" they demanded...

Once more, Marushka made her way bravely through the bitter cold, up to the mountaintop. And once more, she came upon the twelve months seated around their fire.

"Good men," said Marushka faintly, "may I warm myself at your fire? I am so very chilled."

January raised his ancient head. "Come, child. Stand by the fire, and do not worry. Tell us what you seek this time."

"They say I must find red apples," Marushka said, and a tear trickled down her cheek.

January slowly rose and went to one of the young men. Putting the wand in his hand he said, "Good Brother September, won't you take the high seat?"

September jumped up and ran to the large stone. He sat down upon it and waved the wand. The flames rose, orange and scarlet. The snow melted. The forest was filled with the colors of fall. Leaves slowly fell from an apple tree, heavy with red fruit.

"Take what you need, Marushka," said September cheerfully.

Marushka ran to the tree and shook it. Three apples fell. Gathering them, she thanked the months again, and hurried away.

Marushka ran to the tree and shook it.

Holena and her mother were astonished. Grabbing the apples, they shrieked, "Where did you get these?"

"On the mountaintop," answered Marushka.

"On the mountaintop, on the mountaintop," Holena mimicked. "And I'm sure you ate more than you brought too, you greedy thing!"

"No," said Marushka. "I brought back all that I gathered."

"Liar!" Holena shouted. "Leave us now so Mother and I can eat our apples in peace."

Marushka went to the kitchen and wept while Holena and her mother ate all the apples. When they were gone, they both hungered for more, so sweet and juicy was the fruit.

Holena reached for her cloak. "Why should that good-for-nothing Marushka have all the luck? I'll go and get more apples," she said, wiping her mouth and tossing the last apple core to the floor. "We'll have as many as we want."

"I'll come too," said her mother. "That way we can gather twice as many."

So they put on their warm cloaks and each took a basket. Then they set off up the mountainside. Higher and higher they climbed, until they too, came at last to where the twelve months sat.

Marushka went to the kitchen and wept...

Holena went right up to the fire and warmed herself. "We're looking for the tree with the apples," she said. "Show it to us, and we'll give you our servant girl. She can cut your wood and tend your fire." Then she added, "If you don't, we'll report you. You must be bandits, hiding up here in the snow like this."

January raised his head. Frozen tears dropped from his eyes. "Foolish girl. Go home. Apples do not grow in winter."

"Stupid old man!" shouted Holena. "Marushka got apples, we want them too. Give them to us."

January frowned and waved his wand. Overhead the sky darkened. Great flakes of snow began to fall. The fire went out. The twelve months disappeared. Vainly, Holena and her mother wandered in darkness through the dense forest.

Safe and warm, Marushka waited down below. But neither Holena, nor her mother, ever returned.

...Holena and her mother wandered in darkness...

In the spring, Marushka planted twelve seeds from the apple cores Holena and her mother had left. In a short time, a beautiful tree sprouted from each one. The trees grew quickly and blossomed. By September, every bough of every tree was heavy with sweet, round fruit.

Marushka went out and around and invited all her neighbors to come pick apples and share in her harvest.

It was a fine fall day, the sky blue and clear, the air tart and apple-crisp. Men, women, and children came. They picked and picked, and ate and ate. But they took care to leave some apples on the branches and on the ground, so the birds and wild creatures would not go hungry.

Everyone was curious when the twelve strangers arrived. Three were very old men, three were middle-aged, three were young and three — well, three were really still boys. No one remembered ever seeing them before, but Marushka seemed to know them and made them very welcome. And, when the apples were gathered and people came to the tables, they found baskets of sweet-scented violets, luscious strawberries, fresh-baked bread, honeycomb, and frost-cold cider. Music was played, dances were danced, songs were sung. "We must do this again!" Marushka laughed.

"Yes!" declared all the guests. "Let us gather together every year to celebrate the harvest."

Music was played, dances were danced...

I was there too, and took an apple with me from that grand celebration. Only, before I reached home, it fell from my mouth and rolled down a hole — gone! So all I have left to share with you is this story.

But if you don't believe it, why, just come and see! At the foot of our mountain stands an orchard of twelve times twelve apple trees, all in neat rows. Come in the fall when the sweet apples are ripe, and then you too, can join in the party